MAPPING W

Anthology of
Poetry and Prose

S@veAs
writers' group

MAPPING WORDS
Anthology of Poetry and Prose

'Equinox', 'Daffyd's Urn' and 'Hair' by Roger James
all in *Bringing Back the Damsons*
'Déjà Vu' by Patricia Griffin in *Acumen*
'The Wind from the West' by Patricia Griffin in *Orbis*, 2015
'Renewal' by Patricia Griffin in *South 52*
'Ja-Kyung Oh at the Organ' by Derek Sellen in *Poets Meet Politics*, winners' anthology, 2014

British Library Cataloguing-in-Publication Data.
A catalogue record for this book is available from the British Library.

ISBN: 978-0-9929473-9-2

Cover design and editing by Derek Sellen

Typeset and design by
Anna Trussler Design, Totnes, Devon, UK

Contents

Foreword

Formed in 2002, SaveAs Writers always held their meetings at the University of Kent. Throughout the pandemic, they kept in touch via Zoom sessions.

Mapping Words is the group's third anthology of writing, originally conceived in 2016 when entries for this edition were submitted, but due to unforeseen circumstances are only now seeing the light of day. The only stipulation for submissions was that each piece of writing must have been workshopped at a SaveAs meeting.

Contained within this book are poems and short stories by group members that show raw energy as well as a very high quality of writing.

Writers are never satisfied with their work, always feeling it can be improved even when it is on the page and 'out there'. But a work is never complete because you, the reader, have to read it, embrace it. Make it *yours*. After all, as Barthes said, 'To give a text an author and assign a single, corresponding interpretation to it', is to impose a limit on that text.*

For us, *Mapping Words* is a representation of all that is great about the SaveAs Writers' group – mainly the diverse skill of its members.

Luigi Marchini, *Chair*
SaveAs Writers, 2023

*Barthes, Roland, 'The Death of the Author', *Image, Music, Text*, translated by Stephen Heath, Hill and Wang, 1977, pp.142–48.

Acknowledgments

SAVEAS WRITERS would like to thank Patricia Griffin for vetting all submissions. We would also like to thank Derek Sellen for editing the collection, putting it all together and for the fantastic cover art. Lastly, a big thank you to Anna Trussler for getting it all into print for us.

MAPPING WORDS

EQUINOX

Between sunset on our left and full moon rising directly
    on our right,
two leverets, stronger than spring, leap out, bouncing hip-
    high so we stop the car
and stand watching their Equinox light-explosion as
    children might stare at fireworks,
thumbs in mouth, suddenly not understanding these
    bright colours and clashes.

Whilst we struggle between midnight and the clock-twist,
    missing turn-offs
driving too close, overcome with the machinery of what
    we do, Equinox strides out,
dismissing our strip-lights and white noises, arguing not
    for death but for birth,
changing everything – invisible and wise – even as we try
    to photograph and frame it.

And somewhere, swallows are heading straight at us –
    new stars – released by
one twist of the earth – direct, low then high – the sun
    and moon bouncing after them.

GOING OUT WITH A BANG

The sun crests the horizon, throwing its rays across the drops of dew lying heavy on Arthur Pod's web. From his corner, with limbs tucked up around him, Arthur opens a few eyes blearily, then snaps them shut. The dew is dazzling and hurts his head.

He searches for the day. Saturday, please let it be Saturday. But last night comes back to him slowly. Last night was Sunday night. He had gone down The Black Widow for a few with James and Rich. From the animosity he feels towards the bright dew balls this morning, he surmises that 'a few' turned into a few more. He can recall some of the walk home with the boys – a couple of legs draped around each other's shoulders, with those remaining employed at weaving them homewards.

And if last night was Sunday, Arthur needs to get up right now because there is a class waiting to be taught. He draws a slow breath in, and opens all of his eyes at once.

Dragging himself along a strand of web to the nearest drop of dew, Arthur bends his head to it and drinks deeply. He can do Mondays. He has done them before. But right now that knowledge exists as little more than a historical fact, and offers little in the way of encouragement. And there remains something else. Something *more* than just a Monday morning. Then the something else comes to him. Today he is teaching sex education.

*

The morning drop-off ritual is in full swing as Arthur reaches the school gates. He makes his way through the mass that is blocking his path, skirting chatting parents, dodging spiderlings chasing each other. He hears his name called a few times, but pretends he hasn't.

'Ooh Mr Pod! Do you have a second to talk about Jennifer's behaviour?'

No he doesn't. She wouldn't like what he had to say anyway.

He reaches the hallway. Third door on the right – his classroom. Nearly there. Passing Mrs Callum's classroom, Arthur glances in. And there she sits.

'Arthur – Just the man I need. Which of these fonts will be better for Tuesday's web safety presentation?'

Mrs Callum sits at her desk, a neat stack of textbooks in her 'marked' tray. She looks like she has been there for hours already. On her PowerPoint she flicks between two seemingly identical typefaces.

'Morning Charlotte. Err – the second one, definitely. Good weekend?'

'It wasn't bad thanks. You should have joined us at the Vine Leaf on Sunday you know. It was fun.'

'I did want to, but I went down the Black Widow first, and you know . . . ' He trails off, suddenly conscious of his hair sticking up wildly where he had slept on it. Which was pretty much all over. He tries to brush some down with a rear leg. It bristles back up.

'Right I'd best just finish up prep for first period.' He says. 'The dreaded sex ed! Are you ready for it?'

'Born ready.' Mrs Callum winks, and returns to her fonts.

Arthur backs out, and enters the adjacent classroom. Sitting at his desk, he releases a breath that he doesn't remember holding in. This was not going to be fun. Of course it is a very important lesson for all spiderlings to learn. Especially with such an absence of fathers. Studies across the country show that teen pregnancy rates dropped significantly after the class was introduced. But it was always awkward. No escaping that.

At least I have a few minutes left to prepare before I'm joined by the horde, he thinks.

In the playground, the morning bell begins its toll.

*

5

'Sir, why have the girls gone out with Mrs Callum?'

'If you were paying attention last week Owen, you would know why. Today I get the joy of taking the first of your sex education classes. The girls are learning separately because they will have different issues to discuss.'

'I don't need sex education sir – I'm already a master. I could teach this!'

'I am sure you could. But as the school have unfathomably failed to recruit your expertise, I will be taking the lead. Let's get on with it shall we boys?'

Arthur rises from his chair and moves round to perch on the front of the desk, facing the class. He feels this gives him a certain approachability that might make things go a bit easier. We're all in this together lads. He props a couple of his legs up on the desk to add to the casual demeanour. The angle is awkward. He takes his legs off again.

'Now when it comes to sex, there are a lot of myths out there. And when you are growing up and finding your feet in the world it can be difficult to know fact from fabrication. Hopefully over the next few weeks we can dispel any misleading beliefs you have taken on board. You should come out of this with a good understanding of sex and procreation, and be well placed to make informed decisions for yourselves. And Owen you will have to bear with us, seeing as you know it all already.'

'Whatever sir.'

'Alright. Let's begin by calling out some of the things you have heard about sex from your mates, or an older brother perhaps.'

Silence. Glances exchanged. A weighing of whether that which is thrown about so casually in the playground should be brought into the classroom, to a teacher.

'Come on boys. The floor is open. Nothing is too stupid.'

'Sir, I heard a girl only gets pregnant if she actually loves you. That's how you know.'

'Thanks for kicking us off Dean. We'll cover that. Who else?'

'I heard girls can only have sex like five days a month.

It's closed off or something the other days.'

'Mark told me you have to have sex for at least 20 minutes before the woman actually likes it.'

'No I never.'

'Is it true that when you have sex, the next day you can't weave your web in a straight line? Coz your legs are knackered or something.'

Arthur smiles at that one. The boys are opening up. Good. He shifts his position slightly. Sitting on the front of the desk is working very well for him.

'These are great, keep them coming. I say great – I am pleased to tell you that every one of these is what I would call a 'sex myth'. Who's next?'

'My brother said that after you have sex, the girl eats you.'

The class erupts in laughter. Mark Apsley claps. Owen Burns mimics a post coital female. 'Ooh thank you big boy . . . GET IN MY BELLY NOM NOM NOM!'

Arthur's heart sinks: And so it begins.

The laughter settles and Owen regains his chair.

'That does sound funny doesn't it? Now . . . ' Arthur pauses, tries to pick the right words.

'I want us to remain calm and sensible while I tell you something important about that last one. I was hoping to come to it a little later in the term, but let's deal with it now.'

Around the room the smiles fade. He has the rare experience of all 17 boys in the class giving him their undivided attention. The collective force of their 136 eyes burns into him demanding truth, the whole truth, and nothing but the truth so help him God.

'On some occasions . . . there is, ah, truth to the fact that following intercourse, the female spider will . . . consume the male.'

The eyes grow bigger. No one moves. Every tick of the class clock reaches Arthur with perfect clarity.

'I understand you will need some time to process this information – and that's fine. The school has an excellent support system in place for any of you who feel particularly concerned. And yes, boys. We certainly did pull the short straw on this one. I'm in the same boat here.'

Mark Apsley raised an arm. 'So I get to have sex once. Then I die?'

'No Mark, it doesn't happen in a lot of cases. You may live to have many . . . encounters. I know a lot of you are missing fathers, (and now you will understand why) but some of your Dads are still around and going strong aren't they?'

A few heads nod. The majority stay unmoving.

'It would be remiss of me not to explain that certain species have a higher rate of survival following the act than others. Some of you have an excellent chance of walking away unscathed. Others will need to take more care. The males of some species face up to a 60% chance of not . . . making it. Where are the redback twins? George, Ian – you need to be especially careful. I know it's not what you want to hear, and life is hard enough with all the ginger jokes, but I would not be doing my duty without warning you.'

The twins exchange glances. Luke Weatherby reaches over and pats George on the back.

'Now here's the good news. There are things you can do to improve your chances. We don't just have to sit there passively. While the jury is still out on whether some practices actually work, others have been proven and used for centuries. I have prepared a series of hand-outs . . .'

Arthur stands, and distributes the papers to the front row.

'Pass these back please. On here you will find a number of recommendations, websites and books for further reading. There is a series of touches that can hypnotise your partner to take the hunger away for just long enough. Others swear by plucking the web a certain way before the act. Almost like a code.'

The boys receive the hand-outs reverently, as if handling ancient manuscripts.

'Next week you have a session with Mrs Diovacci in the

gym, where you will learn a number of dance routines that can be used to improve your chances. And here's an important one boys – the bigger you are, the greater your survival rate. Don't let those gym passes go to waste. Look at page 4 for some basic lifts to help you bulk up. The greatest survival tip is, of course, abstinence. But let's be realistic – none of us would be here if that was adhered to universally. Failing to prepare is preparing to fail. I don't need to stress the importance of putting in some serious revision. Now, we are almost out of time. Are there any further questions?'

Mark Apsley raises a leg. 'Sir, how come you are still here? What's your trick?'

'I have been . . . careful Mark. I don't go jumping into anything without thought. A tactic I thoroughly recommend to you all.'

Through the small square window in the classroom door Arthur spots Mrs Callum peering in.

'Ok – I can see the girls have already finished. It is more straightforward for them. Less questions I imagine. You can come in, girls.'

The door opens and the girls enter. They walk with a new sense of purpose, a swagger in their step that is barely perceptible yet definitely there. As they take their seats around the class there is a lack of the usual hair pulling or flirtatious antagonism from the boys.

'Welcome back girls.'

Arthur glances across to the door, where Mrs Callum still lingers. She meets his gaze and smiles. Then she turns and walks back to her class, leaving his door open. He watches the sway of her abdomen, her slim legs carrying her rhythmically down the corridor.

LIKE A SPIDER

like a spider sitting on a cucumber
i shall sing to you of incandescent rabbits
('i' do not mean
a capital initial)

and you like a woman in a bath by a hedgerow
will scuttle up the closest tree
('i' would say 'god' but) –

o pre-raphaelite pungent bucolicity
hang it on the road
say – shall we?
you like my song?

I'm the bad sheriff of Nottingham
(majesticules)
i sit around all day in a tree
– Sherwood Forest -
i drop atom bombs
on all the passers-by
– Sherwood Forest –
and they throw – grrrsplunge –
guided missiles at me

like D.D.T.
and o o o that myxomatosis
just like bicycles in the by-way
if i had nine i'd hang 'em loose
jolly jolly
t.s.e. easily coming &
gone
pwoofff!
and up yours eight-legs

don't you wobble your long teeth at me
you bum-ulcer
pwoof!
and up the glen – gone

PATRICIA GRIFFIN

DÉJÀ VU

In the stillness of morning
time pauses – caught
between distorted shadows
                          and long rays of the sun.

It creeps along silken threads, joining
roses with honeysuckle-bine – their scent
fills the pockets of years – meanwhile
time idles, leans on a wall of the house.

In the heat of the day, time
bounces off the concrete paving, dis-
appears into a swirl of dust around
sheds with a stench of rubber and oil,
at a wharf, snakes like the ropes around bollards, waits
for a ship to return.

In the quiet of evening, time lingers
on a jetty, water slap-slaps at its sides;
the sky is neither blue nor black
and through the haze a ferryman drifts
across patches of light and dark water.

At night, time hangs
like a coat on the door,
that snicks open a crack;
a knife-edge of light sneaks
into boxes, secrets are exposed
as present mixes with past,
until the sun chases the darkness –

in the stillness of morning.
time pauses

AKA

Multi-faceted, magical, masterfully
misunderstood, maladjusted. Mesmerizingly

artistic, articulate, amazingly
aggravating, annoying. Astoundingly

devoted, dedicated, delightfully
disruptive, dangerous. Deliciously

MAD

A WALK WITH WORDS

*Inspired by a Natural World programme
about the Essex countryside, presented
by Robert Macfarlane*

He throws a spotlight on rusty
cranes, a prism of appreciation.
Bunches of red berries stretch out,
bounce and catch a blackbird's eye.

Yellow and blue curls decorate
black letter tags, a manifesto
that lives on the sea wall
next to orange circles of lichen.

A lorry, gaping pockets, stock-still
where wheels had moved over miles,
strangled by brambles, returned
to the earth in a shroud of wet leaves.

Bluebells melt into each other
as they dance across a wooded stage
in delicate costumes with perfume
that casts us into the spell of Spring.

Inky pother rises from a tall chimney,
predicts a dismal future. Six miles
above us is all we have left.
Then our voices will be spent.

Violets, stubby and perfectly formed,
sprout every year, bold as summer.
Tread on them and their scent rouses us
to the ways and want to walk with words.

EROSION

The old pub has descended into the drink.
Inglenook extinguished, the bar wall leans drunkenly
waiting for the next slosh of brimming froth.

The church has dissolved into an unholy sea.
The altar stripped, the stoop scoured, the entombed
    reburied
without service or salvation in unconsecrated depths.

The school's out under a timetable of tides.
Graded down by a landslide, no lessons learned;
fish play where chalk can write no rules.

The manor house has fallen to the uprising.
Offered no defence to the unruly waves,
overrun and helpless as the defeated land retreats.

The coastal road ends abruptly.
Our terraced cottages now detached, our gardens water
    features,
bite marks where once we drank and ate.

Omnivorous oceans, insatiable seas.
Your rumbling tides of hunger are picking the coast
    clean,
unsettling our land, despoiling the map, rewriting
    natural history.

A chalk block drops, and a point becomes a face.
It falls, caves in to arches, blowholes, stumps.
Now a toe on the running sands,
now in the water –
gone.

FOX AND HOUND

something just but not quite
out of sight snagged my breath
mis-stepped my intent to slip
through your fine swing door
to become someone new again

or was it the sound of your shadow
across a perfumed lawn newly cut
fronting a fancied home I may yet
surprise with the sharp crease of a smile

I slide again inside my head to those
tumbled days of whiskey sweat
and the shirt off my back for a shilling
gambled in the ghetto streets

and you window-shopping for thrills
cool with your handbag of dreams
while I trailed your scent of fox
like a Laelaps to the stars

TREES ON FIRE

The trees are alight in autumnal shades;
distant wood-smoke twists in the lifeless air,
reminding me of another fire –

the sun had glared at the Earth,
sucking water through every plant, parching

the soil, matted with crisp, curling leaves
and brittle twigs that snapped beneath the feet,
splinters of glass were pierced by spears of sun
until everything was smouldering.

Flames – yellow, red – quickly fed and grew
into a writhing army that licked and kicked
across the ground with increasing speed,
ran amok, jumped ditches, changed direction
at the whim of the wind, walloped and devoured all it touched.

Birds and animals raced from the roaring heat
that became a blazing wall of whirling fire-spirits.
Rations depleted, they lost their strength, shrank
beneath smoke, blanketing a battlefield of red-black wounds:
charred tree kilns, cattle stumps, and that lingering stench of carbon –

fuelling beauty in the process of regeneration.

OCTOBER

A particular stillness; soft and echoing musk
of spice-tang leaf and turbulent wood-smoke stain;
sudden somehow dusk is now, with the fall of dew
unseen in the air, but felt in a dense sense of chill.
Violet and amethyst, the mist
soft-fingers the stubble slopes
threads thickening strands between the darkening trees.

Shock-loud, the pheasants' sudden fireworks burst
like sputtering squibs, flare-stuttering catherine wheels;
castanet cannonades; fierce fields of fire, a furious stage
of claim and counter-claim; a dusk-echoed rage
of boundary, ownership, battle and defeat.

Fury to threaten worlds. Peace, heroes all:
November's greedy guns
will pierce your finery, snatch you to early sleep
your poppy wattles strewn in silent heap.

THE WIND FROM THE WEST

When Willy-Willy howled,
you closed the doors, shuttered the windows,
rolled wet cloths to plug the gaps
waiting for the devil to come.

Red dust swirled like a cup of smoky fire,
spilling over from desert to farm,
crept through every crack,
marked everything it touched,
                              Then vanished,
leaving you to restore the homestead.

Layer upon layer of dust
has settled – tired arguments lost
for ever.

The brightness is hidden from me,
like your fear of Willy-Willy returning,
because you, caught unprepared,
were spirited away.

'*Willy-Willy/Dust Devil*' *the Australian Aboriginal name for
a whirlwind.*

MAJESTIC RIVER

On Wordsworth's description of Coleridge speaking

How well he maps your words
   from their tumbling source,
      your imagination's broken dam
       flowing unrestrained to form
        a majestic river coursing
          from your tongue, *sometimes*
          concealed by forest,
           sometimes lost in sand,
meanders too long for any but you to pursue,
jaunting from sight at the pace of thought
        then flashing out   broad and distant,
turning back on itself inquisitively,
       cutting incisively into resistance,
     dashing   against   rock,
    leaving listeners
   to make what
   they will
   of the splinters –
    his discourse always a stream,
    always a connection
     between its parts
     and his own mind,
      not always perceptible
      to the minds of others –
     not knowing how
     or when to stop;

      to that torrent
      I add
      this
       drop.

ALLEGRA

– loosely based on incidents in the life of Percy Bysshe Shelley

You'd like a Gothic tale? Let me tell you one. We need hardly stray from real events. We end at a churchyard in Harrow but we begin at a nunnery near Ravenna on an August day in 1821.

The convent is a tall, enclosed building with a louring gateway and a weighty door. Yet the inhabitants are not so forbidding as you might imagine. This is not a dark place except in its architecture.

A game of hide-and-seek is going on across the lawns. Some cypresses, a maze of small hedges and a dilapidated outbuilding offer opportunities for concealment. The young man, bright-eyed, with unruly hair and a long straight nose, flits from tree to tree looking for his partner in the game, a four-year-old girl, almost five. She wears a simple white blouse under an apron and little black silk trousers; no shoes, she has kicked them off. There is a gold chain around her neck, a present from her visitor. The nuns are napping before the afternoon needlework sessions.

He moves like a puppet on loose strings. He is thin, on the edge of emaciation; the girl has named him as her paper uncle, her zio di carta. For someone so insubstantial, he has a surprisingly robust history of love-making and travel and physical pursuits. He has indeed spent much of his life (he is barely twenty-nine) among paper – the pages of books, the sheets of his own essays and poems, summonses and letters demanding the payment of debts.

He catches sight of the child. 'Allegra, I see you,' he calls.

'You don't see me,' she shouts in Italian and runs away across the patchwork of light and shadow, like a gaming piece on the move. He could capture her if he tried but he swoops around her as she evades him by twisting and turning, giggling and screaming and yelping with the fun of the hunted. They form two concentric orbits, one of pursuit and one of flight, the first gradually closing on the other.

The nearer he comes, the more her cries become shrill and desperate. She breaks free from the circle and heads towards the outbuilding. He is so caught up in the game that he doesn't realise the sudden change in her mood. There is a bell-rope in the dark doorway. She yanks on it urgently.

The deep-toned alarm bell echoes through the hot afternoon.

Nuns wake and hurry from the convent. The heavily draped women in black enclose her, accusing him with their eyes. He spreads his arms in protestations of innocence. Allegra rests her chin on one of the protective arms, eyes flaming, and shouts to him. 'I don't want you! I want my papa. I want my mammina. Tell them to visit me, *zio di carta*.'

Neither will come; one, her mammina, the Contessa, is not really her mother at all – that is distant Claire, forbidden to visit – and the other is too busy with his pleasures, his writings and his menagerie.

Her face is running with tears. But perhaps she is more furious than scared or sad. The nuns take her away and the visit is ended.

She is twice-named, Alba and Allegra. She doesn't remember the first, given at birth, but perhaps the fact of her two names makes her more of a spirit, less firmly anchored in her body than she would be by one. She is caught between two languages too, an almost forgotten English that sometimes surfaces through her Italian prattle like a ghost.

Both names at the propitious end of the alphabet.
Alba. Dawn.
Her true mother, Claire Clairmont, had named her that. The opening of a day, of a life.
Allegra. Happy.

Her father had chosen that when she passed into his custody.

The partner in the hide-and-seek is not her real uncle; it is as difficult to sum up his relationship to her as it is to explain her place in the world generally. Alba/Allegra, we might say, is only vaguely defined, a sprite rather than a daughter. A small boat, loosely moored.

Allegra dies at the convent less than a year later. Typhus.

The scandalous British father who has rarely visited her blames the nuns for their lack of care. 'My Allegrina,' he laments, suddenly remembering all her childish chatter before he banished her. Even her deplorable wilfulness becomes charming in memory.

Her life in the palazzo had been chaotic, with monkeys and exotic birds running free in the hallways and on the stairs. She had been one more palace cat, cute but liable to scratch, until she was sent to the nuns to be calmed. In her tantrums, she had screeched and bared her teeth, another monkey. She had wandered after the inquisitive Great Egyptian Crane at inopportune moments into private rooms. She is missed now as a beloved pet is missed.

Her zio di carta is equally distressed, perhaps more. His life and Mary's life have been blighted enough by the death of infants, legitimate and illegitimate, miscarriage and stillbirth, fever and convulsions.

Was the Contessa sad? We don't know.

When the news arrives, Claire screams. The unearthly scream of a mother who has been barred from her baby and whose existence was centred on seeing her again.

Shelley, the paper uncle, *does* see her again.

The burial is a difficult affair. It is her father's whim to have her interred in England. In Ravenna the tiny corpse is packed into a lead casket which in turn is placed in an oak coffin which in turn is loaded onto a cart before, at the end of a long journey through several provincial jurisdictions, each requiring its own paperwork, it is taken on board a ship and unloaded again at Dover. In Harrow, the heavy burden is dragged up the hill to the church.

But the vicar baulks at giving graveyard room to a bastard girl. Finally, she is laid in a hole in the ground but no headstone is allowed. Is she therefore even properly buried? A superstitious person versed in Gothic novels might think that, passing through lead and oak and turf, she may rise again.

Even if you are not given to fancies of that sort, you might find Shelley's hallucination disturbing, eroding the foundations of your mundane reality. It comes to him shortly after he hears of her death. Shelley has long believed in spirits and demons. There has been the added pressure on his mental state of the cluster of deaths that he seems to attract.

It is a warm Italian evening in late spring, a crescent moon. There are white frills of surf all along the curve of the bay, each small wave erasing the last. Shelley has just stepped onto the veranda of the beachside house at Lerici when with a high-pitched gull-like cry he points out to sea:

> *A child rises out of the silver tide, as if she has been hiding under the water waiting for him to appear. It is Allegra.*
> *A small girl with a halo of moonlit hair and a gold chain around her neck. She smiles at him, laughs, claps her hands and beckons.*
> *He stands transfixed but the sea comes to him. It floods over the edge of the terrace and rises up his legs, ankles, shins, thighs, as far as his waist. He tries to wade towards her, reaching out both his hands to touch hers, but the weight of water makes it impossible to move.*
> *A heavy wave knocks him off his feet. He is unsure whether he is drowning in brine or in ink, it is so black all around him . . .*

He begins to wake from the trance and finds himself stumbling to the ground. He is dry; the sea is beyond the terrace and the narrow strip of sand, in its proper place and calm, exactly as it should be. There is a bell tolling. This is not surprising. In Italy there is always a church or a convent or a monastery at hand with a knell. However, it takes him back to the nuns' garden and the game of hide-and-seek. Still in the power of the hypnagogic vision, he hears her voice.

'Catch me. Hold me. Keep me.'

'Allegra . . .'

'You see me, *zio di carta*. You see me, don't you?'

'I don't see you.'

He tries to discern her but she has vanished from his mind. Dawn and happiness have vanished, leaving little to live for.

*

You know what happened afterwards. The boating accident in the Gulf of Spezia, the cremation on the beach, the other death in Greece.

Accident? The boat was under full sail in a storm. The captain of a more stable craft offered to take him and his companions on board but Shelley refused either to leave the boat or to take in sail.

There was no record of the final moments. If Shelley cried out and pointed – 'the Child!' – or if he heard her bubbling laughter in his ears, nobody survived to tell it. His body appeared ten days later, his face and hands worn away by his time in the sea.

For more than a century at Harrow, at unscheduled times, the church bells would ring unaccountably, as if their ropes were yanked by a furious infant. The manifestations only ceased when a memorial was placed on the unmarked grave, naming her:

Allegra,
daughter of Lord Byron
and Claire Clairmont

DAFYDD'S YRN

These bells tell me nothing of you,
still in your own ninth circle, following a path
I could never reach on some magic island
where your iron boils out of deep trenches.

I still struggle in your sea-nets, one of your
catches, decked and drubbed, acting out
your talking head, with no time for bankers
or public schoolboys trotting out their platitudes.

This midnight pain in my belly will not do.
It's time now for me to stand with you ash-urn
above the western cliffs, facing our ancestors,
and scatter your remains to set us free.

VIRTUAL MEMORY

Remember the time we went to Beaulieu
as Us? We laughed at the sign 'a la Beach'
because we'd just finished our French degrees.

Remember? We made friends with a dog
who brought us pebbles
in a game of throw that went on for hours.
We kept all those stones, and took them home
I think.

I've got my own dog now,
five horses, six step-kids, and a wife.
My dog's called Kite.
Anyway

when my father died, I took his ashes to Beaulieu
because he'd said he wanted to be set free
in a 'nice place'
and he was very fond of you, my Dad.

You do remember Beaulieu
don't you?

*

No, I don't recall any of that,
my fingers reply,
but I'm so sorry to hear about your loss.

Later, when I switch off for the night
I remember your father's white-silk scarf
we both loved so much, and ponder
the bowlful of stones by my bed.

FRAGMENTS

Through the blurring window pane
tyres on the wet road hiss
shearing oil-stains to rainbows.

Rose hips and berries, blackbirds
flicking leaves, brief arrows
nipping the long brown of winter.

Fading stains on the old armchair
by the cold fireplace, charity bags
of your shoes and clothes.

AT HASLEY

'Wait for me . . .'

My mobile connection is broken as the train jolts to an abrupt stop. Sunshine filters through the window. A blob of light, reflected from my wristwatch, trembles on the table before me. I peer through the dusty glass. We're at a station. Why? This is the non-stop Express to London; I've paid extra for this service. I'm in a hurry to meet someone.

An announcement is relayed: 'We apologise for this train's unexpected delay. It may be for some while.' The automatic doors open.

There's a disgruntled murmuring; people rustle newspapers, fiddle with laptops. Some of us decide to stretch our legs on the platform.

This is an old rural station; I'm surprised it hasn't been demolished. I feel strangely nostalgic; it reminds me of—. I can hardly believe what I see: HASLEY is written on a board in front of a steel spike fence. It used to be a paling one, painted cream and red. Jimmy and I used to hang around here train spotting. When one arrived we'd sneak past the porter to avoid buying a platform ticket. Now there's no one manning the office, no one tending geranium filled boxes. Instead, tall dry grass and willow herb have grown rampant along the fence, and seeding in the cracks. The sun's heat bounces off the concrete. I dab at the sweat on my face, but the next minute I shiver in a brief swirl of air.

Fellow passengers, puffing on cigarettes and checking the time, pace the platform. The glum-faced engine driver and guard lean against the train. I stroll in that direction.

There's an uncanny quietness; quiet enough to hear birds singing.

I stand at the platform's end, recall the day I last stood here . . . 50 years ago? I check on my watch – June 13th – yes, exactly 50 years ago.

*

Jimmy and I were going to London for the day. He'd gone to buy a bottle of Tizer from the buffet on the opposite platform. 'You wait here,' he'd said.

He was taking ages. When I heard the train coming through the tunnel I decided to go without him because I didn't think he'd get across the bridge in time.

'Jimmy! I'm getting on this train,' I called.

'Wait for me!' he yelled back.

The train squealed into the station, steam gushing from the engine. Porters were shouting and scurrying. People leant from carriage windows, opened doors, and asked one another what was going on. A voice crackled through the tannoy.

And then it became quiet for what seemed an endless moment. I stood on the platform watching red liquid dribble from a broken Tizer bottle. I remember hearing a blackbird sing.

I look at the signboard where a blackbird is perched. I hear the driver say 'I swear I saw someone run across.'

A flurry of smoke from someone's bonfire drifts across the track. The blackbird 'tchacks' and flies away in alarm.

'I did wait for you Jimmy,' I whisper.

FRAME

He is lost
my father's father.
                        Lost

before my father's birth
but still here hanging
sepia in a silver frame.

Dressed in trench khaki he stands
shoulders back and smiling.

He has my eyes.

I look into them to hear
the distant rattling of battle

to reach for the far reaches of no-man's-land

to peer stretch-necked
over war's parapet and into his life.

I see him moving now
duck-boarding through sludge
muttering a war mantra
a prayer to deaden fear.

He mounts the fire-step
then the sniper
the bullet in the brain
the evacuation of the gut
the falling back

          mud to mud . . .

                        Lost
yet found again in the mind's mists
strolling through timely meadows
to make his way into my frame
where I have his eyes.

TOMMY

there but for thrum of time
broken rhythm
quirk of date
accident of birth
go I

there but for rush of blood
flock of crowd
goading prod
pressed white feather
go I

there but for brawn
measure of man
ring of lung
curve of arch
go I

there but for conviction
wanting ear
conscription
literate cross
go I

there but for choice
need
desperation
wish
go I

aren't I
the lucky one?

VULCAN

The wedge that drives humanity apart
is not, in itself, this metal wedge, rust-resting now.
No. The furnace where this sleek shape was forged
is the hot unforgiveness of the human heart,
the pride, the lust to claim; boundaries
inside the mind, blind-graven on the ground,
formed this destroyer, this soul-splitter,
    this boundary-breaker
with its predator roar:

                 and yet not tooth, not claw
but the terrible seed, silent cased: whole cities
   laid waste
in a dandelion's puff; ghost globes, blown apart,
dematerialised; erased.

Freighted with boldness and dread, the crews waited;
the call never came; the fear abated.

The shadows of children play
against a sunlit wall.
The readiness is all.

'76

July was a scorcher, the hottest one on record for yonks and yonks. We'd walk to the Spar for Ice Poles, but the rush on them meant they were seldom frozen solid and hardly lasted across the green before turning to luke-warm slush in our hands. If you bit their seal too zealously, you wore a lime green or scarlet grin like The Joker for a couple of days. When mooching about, we tried to burst tar bubbles with our bumpers, but Davo nearly lost his on Birchwood Avenue, and only us lying across the roasting pavement, hamming up the quicksand rescue scene from *Ice Cold in Alex*, stopped him from bursting into tears at the thought of his mum's reaction.

To retreat from the sun we beat it towards our woods, The Backs, so called because they were behind our side of the street. Grabbing our bikes from out front, we did a circuit through the allotments, passed Mr.Ginger's ramshackle shed, each giving it a swift kick as we went by. The sound of ringing corrugated iron echoed across the nettles like a tower clock with the winder slack.

In the shade of the trees we carted hard-core to the foot of The Run, arranging the bricks and chunks like a set of steps, before I dragged dad's missing cement board out from the under-growth and laid it on top. Sweat dripped from my forehead onto the grey mixing stain like that slow motion drop of milk on TV. Wiping my face with my shucked T-shirt, I sucked the deep graze on my knuckles from earlier that day, when I'd come off my bike outside number 13.

Right now, despite being skanky in my muck-around clothes, I stood in my best, very obviously Steve McQueen-couldn't-give-a-shit attitude, and waited. For most this summer, especially Jamie and Davo, this was an Evil Knievel

moment, wrapped in a borrowed bed sheet and pretending
to be their white suited hero – their chance to shine. They
were always ready to leap their version of double-decker
busses – our choked and stagnant, orange-foam stream –
with all the grace and style that a Chopper could deliver.
For me, I was Hilt, the Cooler King from *The Great Escape*,
forever hacking around our estate, evading paperboys,
Nazis or prams left, right and centre, albeit on my third-
hand post office bike, with its blocks on the pedals.

In The Stonehousers, we had no real attempt at
leadership, our occasional pecking order being based on
whoever had the most popular idea or loudest arguing
voice won the day. Consequently, in our scheming or footie
commentaries, I usually became the master of ceremonies
by warrant of having the biggest gob. So, this day I stood to
one side of The Run and shouted for silence. Deciding to
give the littlest kid first crack at jumping glory, I signalled
Ali to the line I'd just stick-scratched in the bank and raised
my hand for silence. And as I did so, I saw him.

Just down the slope from the start line, but about ten,
twenty yards back, someone was behind our swing tree.
Brown granddad shirt undone, blue cut-down jean shorts
and tan desert boots. In the shadow under the ivy I could
only just make out that his hair was quite fair, like a dirty
blond, and that he had a very obvious tan mark where his
collar should be, above a puny white belly.

But the most striking thing about him was that his shorts
were around his ankles and he was wanking, his hand and
groin a blur of action as he frowned, concentrated, staring
straight up the slope – at us.

PERV! WEIRDO! WANKER!

The words came out of me as if disembowelled, my throat
ripping from the panic scream. And for the briefest of
moments, the world stopped. Then all hell broke loose.

*

Jamie, Davo and the boys swung around to where I was
involuntarily pointing, and started yelling too. Poor Ali

35

slumped, scared and uncomprehending to his nine year old knees, dropping his bike in the puddle of pee that rapidly spread around him. Down the slope, the perv was struggling to pull up his shorts, falling over in the process. As he went down, Richard threw a rock at him and, more from fear than anything else, we all followed suit. As fast and as hard as we could, we pelted stones, bricks and sticks at the man as he attempted to shield both his groin and head at the same time as pull on his clothes.

I shot across to the boys, grabbed at Ali's collar, dragging him to his feet. Between us we scrambled back up the slope and ran like shit, taking the long way round through the flats, as the perv was still between us and our houses. Davo was just ranting, Fuck. Fuck. FUCK! over and over again, and someone else said that we must have hurt him, cos he hadn't got up. But by the time we rounded the corner into Stonehouse Drive, we were all silent, spooked by what had happened, by how close we'd come. And then from in front of the garages parents and siblings came running, and with them came Mum with Little Dean on her hip.

*

After a mad, frantic blitz of questions, shouting and tears, the mums led us off into Mervyn's, so that his nurse wife Rene could check us all for shock. Whilst they pumped custard creams and Robinsons into us, Mrs Campbell took Ali upstairs for a bath, borrowing a *Scooby Doo* T-shirt six sizes too big for when he was dry. Over the next hour we watched *Magic Roundabout* and *The News*, and for once didn't complain that we were the wrong age for either.

After a while, Mervyn called us to the door to say that the police were here talking to the dads and brothers on the front drive. With spades, two by fours and other weapons the men stood surrounded by our retrieved bikes, leant on Mervyn's ornamental well, picked at the pebbledash on his porch. Richard's dad was telling P.C. Jones that they'd all gone to The Backs as soon as they'd heard, and searched through the place with a fine tooth comb, Mateley even

willing his German Shepherd, Bruce, to pick up the scent.
But it seemed that all they'd found was one desert boot,
which Dad was dangling from the end of his crow bar.

As the mums ushered us back into the lounge so we
could calm down before we made our statements, Davo
swore he'd seen blood on his dad's spade, started to say
that he reckoned they must have caught him and smashed
him up. Just as he was trying to get us to guess where
they'd buried the perv, I looked past him, down the length
of the hall, and saw Mum lean into dad's chest. She was
shaking and as she pulled in tighter, Dad was forced to take
Little Dean from her. As he did so, the crow-bar levelled
towards the floor and the boot slipped off, landing with a
dull, rubber plop. It didn't bounce, just lay there limp on its
side, as if staring out between the crowd's legs.

RITUAL (THOSE WERE THE DAYS)

O ff the playground slewing grit ever onwards in toe-capped troughs, face burning from thirty minutes righteous singing to end a day of plasticine and slippered whacks, towards sanctuary in a hug. Then shoulder to waist and out the gate in palm-palm grip to cross the road where Leroy's brains once glistened under tyre. On tarmac there's no black or white, only shades of grey.

Up the hill and past the Custard House with midget door which sometimes popped, its scary owners scurrying out – one beard, one skirt, but matching macs. Locking up and going on their wonky wheeled way tartan trolley – big enough to hide a third in, if there was one – bumping off the kerb.

At The Corner, ever wary, Mrs Hobson never came from out behind her counter cage, in case us rats, we fag-end kids stole her out of house and home. So I chose without touching Sherbert Fountains, Curly Wurlies, then you pointed through the wire and the string pulled magic key rose tarnished from between her molten layers of nylonned flesh. Peanut Brittle scent and sweat cloyed to our hair as the door rang closed.

In weather without iced paths or downpours and that sudden hail that pinged off a Parka like bullets off a rock, we'd got to The Park and you'd take the weight off on the third bench read *Woman's Own* stories or watch the swans beak the weed for bread not thrown yet.

And I'd run as Champion the Wonder-Horse, this mighty cannon-ball of childhood, a mass of sugared up, Silver-Top, scabbed on flesh. All Life was in my swoop between the pines, down that slope to where all that separated me and water were your shouts, sometime rails and lucky heels.

When the light was failing or the Sunblest half floating in
swollen pieces at the drain-off, *Time to Go* would come again
and I'd be called to side. Before we walked, you'd shoulder
bags, pocket papers, make me show you hands and just in
case wash mine in the iron spring, take a sip like icy blood
for the journey home.

Once I left my pants there in a bush, a knot of dirt, too-
late, and Dock leaves wondering as we stepped out – like
mis-matched lovers or Jehovas – whether the mongrel Lassie
from nearby flats would follow with a wish to embarrass, Y-
fronts between its teeth. That night I asked for a bath though
it wasn't Sunday, and you picked yourself off the floor long
enough to run it and quiz me softly, softly whether I was
alright, my paisley jim-jams seeming to scream from the
radiator *Don't tell her – or there'll be no T.V.*

Most nights, only homework punched a hole in my sky.
Early days, Peter and Jane butted their shiny faced way
between me, sofa and tea. And later, a trench X foot wide,
Y foot deep, two trains colliding, or the mess of probability,
put a dent in my right to draw castles and spacemen. Ziggy
and Slade in the other room, guitars through the wall tugged
at sulk elbows on the un-laid table. Face to the cool kitchen
lino between ideas, nose full of Heinz Beans, Birds Eye, and
Toast-Topper-vomit from under the grill. Tea, *Nationwide,*
teeth and bed – much of a muchness, ritualistic and lovely.

SECOND BORN

Suck the end tight,

thread, pierce and pull.

My Mother sewed my sweetness into her fabric,
beaded frocks with flouncy frills,
beribboned golden locks
framing faraway sky eyes.

Sewed away the grief
for her chocolate eyed Gerald
lost at 18 months, to the
thread, pierce and pull.

And so, in turn, I
softened the shell-shocked fright
of a war torn childhood, with the
soothing, circular rhythm of

rolling balls from old wool,
unwinding, rewinding
to the clickerty clack of the
in, round, through, out.

I knitted myself a teacher's gown,
secure in its warmth.
Enjoyed the simple, steady repetitions
of tables, sums and drills.

I knitted a husband into my soft vest,
points of course red twine with sulphurous flecks,
relieving the monotony of soft cream, curled
shapeless at the edge.

I knitted three children into my fabric,
bright clashing colours.
Covered disharmony
with blue and red homogeny.

I knitted garments for the grandchildren,
unworn, unappreciated.
but continued still, with the
calming harmony of the

in, round, through, out.
Beany hats for sick babies
Red, yellow, green.
Mittens, jumpers, booties and blankets

Gifts for the innocent
angel eyed, chocolate box
babies that we once were,
that they are now.

TREVOR BREEDON

SECRET AMBITION

In my first years of striving
towards your secret ambition,
I could never understand why you hated your job;
bent over books, I imagined
plunging through darkness
in a cage full of ragged adventurers,
helmets, knee pads and boots jostling,
snap tins hanging like spare ammo packs,
armed for the unknown, on a journey
not quite to the centre of the earth
but deep and hot enough.

I could never fathom your hours;
you were a blanketed shape on the settee
while we ate in considerate silence
and the dark morning rattling of the poker
on the fire grate as I lay in bed tracing
the ritual in my sleep: the twisting of
newspaper knots, the stacking of coal,
middle pages of the Mirror spread
and scorching against a standing shovel
to draw the roar of flames
up the chimney past my head.

I never saw your white smile break the grime,
the shot the cameras always caught;
'Don't bring dirt or work into the house'
was your rule. The day you returned
in shock after the roof fall, I knew
darkness and danger had tunnelled too deep
to end my fascination; when you carried home
the black polished fossil imprinted
with the perfect image of a fern
I saw the reflection of its beauty in your face
and the pride in a job you could never admit.

THE CIRCLE

I'm eleven, in second hand khaki and cut down shorts. Crawling away, backwards through the field grass like Cool Hand Luke on the run from a chain gang. Out of sight. I've got to the count of a hundred until the others come looking, but they'll rush the numbers as ever, so when I've crossed the ditch and am safe in the tree line, I'm off at a half stoop, ripping through the hazels, bow at the ready, dart tips for arrow heads. Ferns shoot spores into the air as I bang past, happily half blinded by the strobe like effect of shadow, light, shadow, light of a high July sun. Behind me I can hear the cat calls of Lee, Kristian, Terry – whooping Sioux, desperate to string up this boyhood Richard Harris. Run, run, run. A rabbit scares me as much as I do it, stuck for the briefest of seconds, trembling amidst the hoof tracks, but gone before I let fly a shot. Shrugging it off as a chance missed, I bound down the slope, jump poorly, splash silt from my baseball boots onto those giant bog leaves as I go. Up the hill, to the sound of the pack, voices high and taunting. Take a sharp left and a zigzag path through brambles, the smell of wild garlic in the air. Onwards – across, under, round still going strong. 'Til – whack! I trip on some log, in some rabbit hole, and I'm pitched headlong, down, head over heels, bow ripped from my hand, arrows busted. There's a spinning, jarring roll and I thud to a halt, flat on my face, and lie there, eyes closed, winded.

After a while recovering, I realise that there's nothing broken, 'cept my skinned knees, and lie listening to my heart thump in my ears. Shortly, I roll onto my back, wondering why the gang's voices have silenced, waiting for the sun to hit my face. But it doesn't come – so I open my eyes for a quick look-see. Here in the belly of the wood, I'm in a hollow. There's winter leaves still on the ground, black, brown and damp. To the right of my hand there's a log covered in orange fungi, moss over sides, smelling sour. The canopy above is tightly woven, hardly breached by the sun. As I twist round onto my knees, what light filters through seems to be reflected back from what look like large butter-flies or ribbons of pink, white, brown stuck amongst the branches on the edge of scene. I try to shake my head into focus and the half-light yields something to me. A circle of magazine pictures, pages, torn apart and photographs sneaked, developed, chosen, dissected, brought here. As I stand I see thorns and sticks punching holes in paper, piercing buttocks, thighs, faces into place, and I grasp that I am smack in the middle of a ring of porn. That someone has taken an age of time, a huge effort to put it here. To arrange it just like this.

And then I realise that all the eyes looking back at me are those of children.

LEARNING TO BREATHE

(*A Lyric Sequence*)

1.
When I look at the computer screen
I am the only one of me that does so.
And when I look away, I know that others,
who are not me, do the same.

2.
I think I know why I *am*
and so does she.

3.
The snail crawls out
in the rain.
The locust flies by
in the heat.

4.
Water drops on earth,
the sound of rain,
the sound of blood.

5.
Sometimes when I am underground and lost in the
perilous honeycomb of warrens and worming tunnels, I
emit a double bass of despair. No one hears me, not the
maggots that look for me, nor the rabbits that I can feel
nearby. Do they care for me, these creatures, as I strive
for an exit knowing that somewhere above there is a
different life? That a movement or a gesture across the
ocean could have a consequence here, for me. Right
now. Or for the rabbits and maggots.

They are hungry now I know but I am not afraid.
Instead I discern the clatter of the bones I disturbed not
long ago, muffled by the soil as they grunt and groan to
the sound of water above, and the shuffle of shadows
down here.

6.
mother of all snails
father of all locusts
pray
that we do not drown
that we do not starve

7.
We know there is always life
because when there is none anymore
how would we know?

8.
Can it be that sometimes

the locust flies in the rain
the snail dries itself in the heat?

9.
On the computer I compose letters, check emails, see what
the weather is like in Amalfi, see what my boss's house
really looks like (maybe I shouldn't have!), catch up on
telly; I might get round to watching DVDs like the Kuro-
sawa box set, or the Von Trier (have tried but it's heavy
going) – it really is amazing this computer – but more
importantly I can use Word to write love sonnets whilst
listening to Sinatra or Gaye and I can make it my world.

10.
She thinks she knows why he is
and so does he.

11.
Beautiful children

12.
She asked, what kind of week
have you had? How have you felt?
I replied, ok, I think. Better than
the last.
She said, can you see
the sun through the window?
I said, no, I haven't looked.
She said, oh, oh, oh.

13.
All children are beautiful,
my grandmother used to say,
even if they are born ugly.

14.
When the office is empty,
I switch the computer on,
secretly,
looking round,
making sure
no one else is.

15.
A man asks a woman for a light,
she obliges,
they kiss,
make love –
a hundred years ago.

47

ONE RUMOUR OF YOU

One rumour of you,
like the blur on the edge of sound
the skin-prickling
fore-runner of thunder

like the rippled rings
flowering the pool at dusk
engraving the silver, circle on circle
whose scarce-glimpsed point of origin
– some flick of motion –

betrays

the presence
of the recent past, alive
somewhere concealed, swimming
deep in time-behind-time;
the movement
of the invisible hunter,
the finned muscular swirl
the danger beneath.

The rings on the pool:
an emblem of peace, from afar.
reflection and image meet;
a seamless pas-de-deux, a
perfect-seeming
kiss.

Close to, a surface collision,
the meeting of different breaths.

A savage, simple death.

The unsurvivable greeting,
the recognition,
the bright, impassable mirror;
the boundary between
two modes of existence

which by their definition
can never meet.

HINEMOA, TŪTĀNEKAI AND ME

Tūtānekai's knife frees the flesh from the wet wing
of an albatross so the flight bone shines clean,
then blows the tube dry until the kōauau spirit sings.

I run the knife under the tap, the water curls and spits.

The bird's ancient song soars from the moon-white flute
to the shore where Hinemoa sits with hollowed gourds,
picks stars for Tūtānekai in the spiced green night.

You left in a fit of swearing spite. I peel onions and weep.

She plaits honeysuckle, frangipani, khowai in her hair,
dips the calabashes in Rotorua's languid waters,
tips her head to trap a sea bird's far off call.

I stuff meat in the pot, turn up the heat.

Tūtānekai carves great flutes of wood and stone,
bores wind holes in an ancient moa thigh,
warms against his heart his tribe's ancestral bones.

The phone keeps ringing – your 'sorry's' will keep.

Hinemoa weaves a raft of black mamaku fern,
ties six gourds round her waist with golden flax,
wets her breast in the sulphur's hiss and turns.

I wash my hands, set plates, and sharpen my teeth.

*(Loosely referencing – and sabotaging – the Maori legend
of Tūtānekai and Hinemoa. Tūtānekai uses the spirit of his
kōauau (flute) to entice Hinemoa to cross sulphurous Lake
Rororua to him.)*

THE TRICKSTER

With tower blocks the balance seemed more up than down – every one a slick concrete rocket chance to forge sci-fi communities full of citizens transplanted and Julietting from balconies, set sure to enjoy the surround-sound lark song, and beyond each cockpit's width of glass, wide, Technicolour visions of blue-remembered hills and pure air to breathe far from the hue and cry of dark work-shops, outside lavs and ricket gutters.

Eventually the lift would lay cry to this, its ascender/descender buttons giving false witness to the possibility of higher beings – but something didn't mind any kind of Out of Order for inside lived Otis and back with the first swish and jolts, the nerves and bile threatened throats of the christening crowds, yet soon gave way to repeat riders, concerted rushing to suck in awe, pucker up to wonder. And all the while Otis rode underneath – prone in the cavity beneath feet, black brow pressed flat in the tightness, burnt root nose twisted sideways, sniffing long and hard the Old Spice and Yardley, jaw chudding, teeth bared as poxed tongue flicked the stainless-steel underside clean.

Curling himself tighter around the mechanism, Otis released oil breath and filing spray in a long, shallow huff onto the metal and in his milky sclera eye-line drew a smiley face in the cloud, imagining its flesh as yellow as his iris and widening its sockets pupil dark – then laughed at the squeals above and as the lift jerked, gears clicked, curled out a mischief smile.

Later the new-dream-sheen wears off, portholes on the world rust, condensation pools and black-mould disengages the twitching nets as the collective shrinks from regiment to battalion, through platoon to splinter cells where the clumps and loan wolves squat so close to the plick and hiss of three-bar fires that denim singes, patchouli oil cloys and in amongst the cement cancer hacks and wheezes, feet are stamped, hands clapped and there's a fruitless tapping at the mercury bubble, whilst out on the skywalks, quick tar repairs flake and split into orphaned snakes and stuttering ribbons drip, drip, drip to fill the stairwells below.

Throughout, Otis grows – in times of plunder and doubt lulling himself with every creak and groan, as, skin bog-man taut, he swivels head and rolls shoulders in the gasp between attempt and reason, every bump-dragged pram, curse on stairs or frustrated sigh tickling his funny bone, all punches and kicks on the jammed doors adding vim and charging him down amongst the cables. There he deliberates and at the point of need, dislocates himself from around the gears, positions lips tight around the tamper-gapped nuts and bolts and hoovers the piss, aerosol-bleeds and cum deep into him, picking the matches, johnnies and wrappers from the gaps of his teeth.

When refreshed, Otis hums as he rests palms at the seals above, cracks the knuckles of his trident fingers, and inserts their scratched, syringe thin tips into the stainless-steel plate where they gloop-on like climbers into pointing pug, slowly growing, swelling til bulbous and blister sore as if lancing the very cyst of this place – then injects it back – swollen by wish and spite, chuckling as the spores breed out, out, out. Every high-rise is a world apart with a spirit and life force all of its own – a character,swelling, building.

THE GARAGE

3 am. Fox barking.
The extra money is lovely, but the broken sleep is
  Why not wait until morning? asks Gavin. It's anti-social
using a garage at this hour.
  I'm slipping, trying to catch hold of
  His light goes on, click. He's looking at me, arms folded,
as if wake and sleep are simple binaries.
  Turn off the lamp. I'm begging you.
  Grind, grate, slam. The garage door goes up, then down.
  How delightful, says Gavin.
  There's only so

                 many

           times

              I can

  apologise

                    I'll quit

            the

    contract in

              the morning.

The ad in my stream. It triggered a reflection on how we
were living; our joint income was digging us out of overdraft
each month, but we were little more than
  This isn't fair on the children, I remember. No one would
want to rent our garage. There's no harm in trying. Rent
your garage, earn some extra cash. Charlotte outgrew her
violin last summer. Ruby's football studs are worn to their

screws. They deserve better than we're giving them. It's a simple solution. Christmas sorted for the kids. The result: we don't sleep, the language centre of my brain is shorting out. Our neighbours either side have stopped talking with us.

There never was real conversation, not when it could be avoided. But the recent looks are colder than the morning frost on our cars. It's made worse by them talking with one another.

No doubt we are the subject of their conversations, I say to Gavin.

You can't blame them, he says, our home is a yellow box warehouse.

I log on. Garages-4-Rent will cancel the contract with the client and ask them to drop the keys back. What now? Gavin's stomping will end, he'll quit his blame-filled silence, and our memory of this time can fade.

Smile then, I say.

Four days, the keys haven't been returned and the garage is still being used. All the optimism is folding in on itself, looking back at us with a false grin.

Fuck it, says Gavin, I'm changing the lock.

Let's give it a few more days.

Seven nights of broken sleep are ticked off, on the eighth day there's a locksmith on our drive.

Big problem these renters, says the man. This late-night nonsense is happening all over town.

It's good to know we're not the only ones, I say, embarrassed that he knows our reason for changing the lock. Gavin could've lied or simply not told him.

Inside the garage is empty, swept clean. It doesn't look like the space is used to store anything.

They're tidier than us, says Gavin.

Funny, I say, thumping him in the thigh.

When a car arrives in the night, the boot goes up and some tools are dragged out. In the morning we see the lock, fitted only yesterday, lying on the drive, a new one has replaced it.

Nice waste of time that was, says Gavin.

He wants to talk with the tenants and find a resolution.

Problem: I've no phone number or email address, it was all arranged through the website. Solution: Gavin decides to stay awake for them.

The night is a restless one, I'm worried about the conversation he'll have.

2.56 am, the men arrive, shaven headed and thick necked. I watch through the curtains as Gavin approaches them with an excuse me. They are showing him some papers.

You signed a seven-year contract, he says, when he walks back into the bedroom.

I'm sure that's not right, I say. It was a few clicks.

If we want to sell the house, he says, they still have ongoing use of the garage.

It can't be true, a signature would be needed for something like that.

He asks if there's a printout he can read. There was a series of boxes, I say, and some text to scroll through, nothing else.

It looked fine, that's my memory. *It all looked fine.*

When I speak with the website, they tell me that we're on the enhanced tariff. It's less flexible than the standard one and the cancellation I attempted, that was a bug. The system shouldn't have let me do it.

Gavin's response is to arrange an appointment with a solicitor. I protest at the cost, but he's determined to resolve the situation with the garage. At Pewter, Leghorn and Stock, we're told to all intents and purposes the contract is legally binding.

It will require a strong case to rebut the legality, says the solicitor.

His name is Philip Stock, and he suggests we take some time to think about it, shaking hands as we depart his office.

Gavin would like to proceed, but the cost is beyond us, and so the walk home happens in an angry, disappointed, confused, exhausted cloud of hair-pulling exasperation.

Living on the salary of a supply teacher and an admin, I say, there is no way to afford it.

There is equity in the house, he says.

You want to risk everything, to end a temporary inconvenience?

Seven years doesn't feel temporary, he says.

And the costs?

They'll be covered by the ones in the wrong, not us.

Proving right from wrong takes time, I say.

The alternative is to accept being tricked, and let others be tricked too.

You're placing all the responsibility on us, I tell him, and all the financial risk. The people at fault are Garages-4-Let. They are the monster, not anyone else.

*

The number of nightly visits to the garage increase. It isn't until the early hours that we collapse into sleep each night.

Gavin is short tempered and beaded with sweat. He pulls the sheets from me whenever he turns onto his side. The lack of sleep makes my fingers vibrate and I can't control my body temperature.

The nights hit hard on the morning routine. The alarm fails to penetrate our exhaustion.

Arriving at work late doesn't go unnoticed. By lunchtime the day has been too long. There is no amount of coffee that can fuel my body into mid-afternoon. I'm caught sleeping in the toilet cubicles.

Is everything ok at home? asks Jeff.

Some trouble with the neighbours, I say.

All-night parties? he asks.

I confirm his assumption; it's easier than an explanation. He tells me there were similar problems at his old house. His family were forced to move. The details are a white noise emanating from him. I try hard to snap into focus.

Sometimes it's all you can do, he says.

Rightmove is opening on my desktop. Jeff walks away, coffee mug in hand, satisfied with his advice. The garage might not be a big deal, I try to convince myself, no one really uses garages these days anyway. They might be grateful to have tenants, a little bit of income to help with the mortgage payments.

Gavin says that selling our home would be a surrender.

It's more like a liberation, I say, we could start again.

He lists his objections, but he knows that our love isn't there for the house anymore.

At the estate agents we are greeted by a young man. He introduces himself as Simon and walks us through the process of placing our property on the market.

It can be awkward selling with a tenanted garage, he says, but reassures us that, with the strength of the market, most buyers will overlook it.

It might even be a bonus to some, he says.

An offer arrives at the end of the first week. Simon rejects it without consultation.

Too far below the asking price, he says, you'd be fools to take it.

There is no choice but to trust Simon. He sleeps, and cognitively functions, whereas we do not.

Too much, says Jeff, on Monday morning. This is all too much.

He lists the falling asleep, the spreadsheet errors, the wrong shipments going out, the aggression.

I've tried hard to be understanding, he says, but . . .

Notice is handed to me, and Gavin falls to the same fate on the following day.

It feels horrible to have become liabilities, expelled, sat at home, our bosses don't even want us to work through the notice periods. But this time is not to be wasted moping, we need to prepare the house for viewing.

The interest peaked in the first week or two that the house was on the market but has started falling away to nothing.

This is when the off chancers drop by, says Simon, the people who see the board and knock on your door. It's always good to have the place ready for them.

I tell him that we have two children. There is no way to keep tidy 24/7. He responds by encouraging me to embrace the Zen of eBay and to clear out the junk. It makes me want to throttle him. (This is no empty expression, my fingers tingle with the potential to commit crimes.)

Simon's guidance only makes sense when we've settled into a nocturnal routine and recovered some sleep hours; the reversal of sleep and waking providing the necessary shift to regain clarity.

On the day our last drop of income lands in the joint account, things become real; selling junk is helpful. Once the mortgage restarts it will be crucial.

By the time the second offer comes in, the bank is putting pressure on us to restart our payments. The offer is lower than the first, it will pay off the debts to the bank, but nothing more. The estate agent tells us it would be insane to exchange for the amount offered.

We don't have a choice, says Gavin, the mortgage can be postponed no longer.

Our options shifted so quickly.

It's my fault for not agreeing to legal action, I say.

Don't blame yourself, he says.

It's difficult not to.

Charlotte returns home on the same afternoon that the sale is agreed with a torn blouse and a broken bag. The blouse can be mended with a needle and thread, but the bag is beyond repair.

I walk her down to the charity shops on the high street, but I'm as embarrassed as she is to be seeking a bag among the shelves of discarded items.

The search is hopeless. Retail stores are the only option.

She asks me if I'm sure it's ok.

You can't go to school with a broken bag, I say, mentally putting on hold my next dental appointment.

*

The first thing my new job is teaching me: Rachel creams off the big houses by sitting closest to the door. The woman has an iron bladder, never takes a comfort break. It's only when she's on a viewing that the top-tier houses reach Marianne, her second in rank.

My desk? It's too far from the door to receive anything but the scraps they discard.

Betty, the office secretary, tells me with a wink and nudge that Mr Wither didn't give her the prime position for nothing.

I like Betty, she's brilliant at filling the quiet times, but I believe very little of what she says.

Rachel and Marianne are both out for the next hour, and Mr Wither is in the rear office, so it's just me and Betty. She's asking where I like to go out in town, pubs and clubs, then critiquing each one from her own point of view.

The Partridge, she says, looks like an old man's pub to me.

I ask her where she goes out at night.

Harper's, she says, decent tunes in there, DJ at the week-ends.

I've only seen the place empty.

You need to go after eleven, she says, that's when it gets going.

I'm promising to give it another try when a married couple walks in looking disorientated.

Simon Grantham, I say, extending my hand, as the bell above the door finishes tingling.

Their names are Mr Gavin Smith and Mrs Patricia Smith.

Selling, buying, or letting? I ask.

They want to put their house on the market, so I take them through the checklist to verify their ownership of the property they are wishing to sell.

One thing we should mention, says Mr Smith, there are tenants using our garage.

I ask him if the rental agreement will continue after the house sale.

He confirms it will.

Not a problem, I say, it might even be a bonus to some buyers.

Once the paperwork is done, I suggest we go and take some pictures.

Follow us, says Gavin.

I take a company car, the one that's plastered with advertising. It's small and easy to park; not that parking is a worry on the seventies' estate.

The house is unremarkable, typical of its time. A detached garage, one-and-a-half sized, is angled at ninety degrees to the house. It's middling stock for its age.

The photos don't take long given the property's simple layout. It'll appeal to young families with children. The little ones can play out in the quiet roads and cul-de-sacs.

The house is situated on Rosewater Close, which connects to Poplar Way. I'm trying to connect the logic of the naming, but things weren't as obvious back then. Those were more innocent times before developers had human psychology down to a fine art, or rather an incontestable science.

Mr and Mrs Smith are grateful for the haste with which I've worked and look forward to seeing their property online.

There's a phone call, it's a few days after the property details are posted, an offer for the Smiths' house. It's far too low, and I nearly laugh down the phone.

Betty looks over at me, I make gestures at the phone. It amuses her, but I quickly stop when Mr Wither opens his door, curious at the giggles.

I give my apologies to the caller and tell them that the amount is unrealistic. It's not credible to expect houses to sell for half their asking price.

They mention the tenanted garage.

Rental income should be considered a bonus, I say, rather than a negative.

The caller hangs up, he's unhappy that I won't pass the offer along.

When Mr Withers returns to his work, Betty wants details of the conversation. I tell her it was just someone trying it on.

Lowballing? she asks.

Yeah.

Mr and Mrs Smith drop by the next day.

They are a little upset that I didn't let them know about the offer. I promise next time that no matter how low, I'll pass each one through them.

Things go quiet after this, and I tell them to declutter and make their house ready for viewing at a moment's notice. This doesn't go down too well with Mrs Smith.

We don't have time, she says, half screaming, not with two kids.

I'm not worried. The sellers usually come around and understand that it's the right thing to do in the end. I had the same thing with Mr and Mrs Farleigh, the coincidence was that they were also selling a house with a tenanted garage.

These garages have become a bit of a theme with sellers wishing to employ the services of Taylor & Wilbrox Estate Agents. It could become my specialism, if I can angle the marketing correctly.

Betty puts a call through. It quickly becomes apparent this could be my opportunity. The caller is interested in a selection of properties; a landlord who has made money elsewhere. He's particularly interested in reluctant sellers. There's some theory in his mind about them owning properties they don't want to leave, and so by his logic those are properties others would want to live in.

The buy-to-let clients are always looking for an angle. It's one of the first things that Mr Withers taught me. He told me to stay sharp when negotiating with them, and never get sucked into the emotional or aspirational tosh.

I prefer finding homes for people who want to live in them, but you can't pick and choose in this business. And this could be a major boost to my sales.

The second time the buyer calls, I tell him there are no chains on any of the properties he's interested in. I tell him that he's getting incredible value, in every possible way. I then start working on his pity, revealing small things, but not too much about the scenario of each property owner, hoping he'll raise the prices he's paying, at least a little. I know that it's unlikely in our hardened world, but it's always a possibility that if you rummage around, you'll find a heart.

To my surprise, the technique works in a way that I wasn't expecting. It's like there is an epiphany down the phone line. This is when he starts formulating a plan with me, asking if I will act as a go-between with the sellers. I listen carefully as his idea floods out with ever enriching details and wonder how many more capitalists can be turned into philanthropists by this talent of mine.

It feels like a superpower.

*

You sometimes have to give to get back. Charlotte is now the proud owner of a new (second-hand) violin. Ruby has football boots that fit. I trusted fate that we'd be ok, and fate gave back. The low offer on the house turns out to be something more than an unrealistic buyer: the purchaser has a plan, he is a mission-seeking philanthropist.

What? I shit you not. He wants to rent our house back to us.

The rent will be equal to the funds you receive from the garage, says Simon, and will remain set at this level.

At last, someone is looking out for us, and with every new detail, another kilo of stress is lifted from our chests. A week ago, our life was in ruins and we were without a prospective home. Now our troubles are waved away.

The buyer has no interest in owning the garage, it will remain separate from the sale. He will also give us the option to buy back the house should we find ourselves able to do so, and only for the price he is paying.

*

Yet more luck. The nightly visits to the garage have ended. We're functioning again, and Gavin is offered part-time work. I follow suit on the employment. It isn't long before full-time posts are available to us.

It feels good, says Gavin, so good to be back on top.

The neighbours have sidled their way into a renewed acquaintance. They are curious about our 'For Sale' board coming down and ask what is happening.

The sale fell through, I say, and we've decided to stay. (It's a small lie to cover our embarrassment.)

*

I've lived in Rosewater Close for a decade now. The Smiths have been here all that time. I'd call them a loving family who respect the privacy of their neighbours. That was until the business with the garage.

First there were the nightly noises, then they started acting strangely. Arthur took some photos, in case we needed evidence. Not sure what for, but sometimes you have an inkling that something suspicious is going on, he says. It seems he might've been right.

I tell Mrs McAlister about my recent query to the Land Registry.

They've sold the house for a fraction of what it's worth, I say, and Arthur is worried that the value of our houses could collapse as a result.

Strange, she says. Patricia told me that the sale fell through.

*

There is no delay in arranging with our landlord to buy back the property through a rent increase at first and then a mortgage application once we've been in our new posts long enough to apply.

He's our guardian angel, says Gavin, celebrating our recent luck.

The evening is spent making steady progress through a bottle of Prosecco.

It's unbelievable, I say, the world is not full of shitheads after all.

1 am. The sound of the flap on our letterbox falling after weeks of silence wakes us from the Prosecco's grip. Gavin returns from downstairs with an envelope, inside are photographs of him with our garage tenants sharing a piece of paper. On the back of the images are two numbers: 327 and 328.

There follows a letter three nights later, no doubt the result of frustration at our inability to understand the meaning or intent of the earlier images.

W • E • K • N • O • W • Y • O • U • A • R • E •
U • P • T • O • S • O • M • E • T • H • I • N • G

This is nonsense, says Gavin. If it's not one thing, it's a-bloody-nother.

He seals shut the letterbox flap each night with parcel tape so that nothing can be posted.

An envelope is left on our doormat. There is a demand for money.

S • T • O • P • O • R • P • A • Y • F • O • R • O
• U • R • S • I • L • E • N • C • E

Parasites, says Gavin, I'm going to find out who's doing this.

It's time to call the police, I say, there's no point in stirring things up ourselves.

An officer arrives to interview us.

And why do you think this has happened? he asks.

There were problems with our neighbours a few months back, I say, but all is resolved.

Perhaps one is still disgruntled, he says.

The officer questions whether anyone might've intercepted our bank statements.

I don't think we've seen one for a while, says Gavin, but I'm not sure why that'd matter.

Monday. There is a second policeman on the doorstep.

Good afternoon, Madam.

The officer steps inside the front door and asks if Gavin is home. There is a warrant in his possession for our arrest under the Proceeds of Crime Act 2002.

Is this connected with Garages-4-Rent? I ask.

He knows nothing about a website. I offer to show him, but he's not interested.

The police have gained access to our bank records. Payments in and out of the account are found to be suspicious. There is supporting evidence from our neighbours; CCTV footage and photographs of Gavin meeting with criminals.

Please come with me, says the officer.

This must be a mistake, I say.

The policeman guides us to the small car parked in front of our drive. He isn't listening to our protests of innocence.

Gavin makes his way around the car to the front passenger door, he is absent-mindedly in mini-cab mode, nervous no doubt about making conversation. The policeman is quick to demand that he sit in the back.

*

I'm watching Mr and Mrs Smith being assisted into a small panda car and regret encouraging Arthur in his plan to 'spook' them a little. He'd been wanting to do something all the time the garage noise was going on. I'd told him not to, but then there was the house sale and Mrs Smith's lying about it. This convinced me he might be right, and that sending the photos would make them reverse whatever their plan was, but he got carried away with the project.

It happens when you're retired, he's not really to blame. There are plenty of people like him who would do exactly the same, but this doesn't stop me feeling bad for the Smiths.

I ask him if he knows what will happen to the children, Charlotte and the tomboy, Ruby.

He shrugs.

Mrs McAlister is with me and I feel dreadful that their parents have been taken away by the police.

I'll take the kids a casserole for dinner, I say, to make sure everything's ok.

Save yourself the worry, says Mrs McAlister. There will be grandparents who can call round.

You're right, I'm fretting about nothing.

As always, says Arthur, his feet on the pouffe.

*

Things rarely happen in isolation. If a crime is committed, it is often repeated. And the criminal displays his or her artistry, like any other artist, through variation.

Mrs Francesca Bardel is visiting me with concerns over a contract her husband entered into online to rent their garage.

She is not the first person I have given advice on this matter. She's at least the fourth for fifth. First there were the Smiths and then the Farleighs, and at least two more followed them.

She tells me about her husband.

He was testing the water, says Mrs Bardel, seeing whether anyone would be interested in renting our garage, and before we knew it, he'd clicked agree and tied us into the whole thing.

I tell her that it's a very easy thing to do and ask her what happened next.

On the website, she says, there was mention of a cooling-off period, but they won't let us cancel.

I tell her that having looked into the website for a previous client, the small print advises that the pseudo cooling-off period only applies if both parties agree to it.

You might've agreed, I say, but if the other party hasn't then it's void.

Shocking, she says. None of this was made clear.

I'm sorry for the predicament, I say, explaining how typically, property is exempt from the statutory rights of cooling off and the company has a somewhat odd approach to modifying this.

Isn't it illegal? she asks.

Misleading, but not necessarily illegal.

But a court case, could it overturn the contract, right?

The problem is we don't know the people in charge of Garages-4-Rent, or where the company is based.

Mrs Bardel asks to know the choices available.

I don't want to alarm her but feel it a responsibility to tell her about the recent arrest of Mr and Mrs Smith following their involvement with the same garage letting website. The newspaper is still on my desk, and there's a quote in the report from the estate agent, Simon Grantham. He's twenty-five years old and his photo is featured.

I've met him, she says. He was at The Partridge one night. Someone mentioned they were renting their garage. They were fed up, and it's one of those pubs where people overhear conversations, and everyone joins in.

I mention Garages-4-Let, she continues, others name similar websites, and he approaches us.

*

This sounds like an unusual approach for an estate agent, so I ask her for more detail.

He spoke enthusiastically about having a buyer in place for houses like ours, she says, we'd not even mentioned selling.

It sounds slightly sinister to me, I say.

The drink had heightened his confidence, and he seemed very ambitious, she says. I'm not sure sinister is the word.

I talk with her about how the nicest of men can end up being the most awful people.

This young man could be the frontman, I say, or at least legally interpreted as the frontman for a fraudulent operation. His approach in the pub triggers my suspicion in particular.

She sits recalling the conversation, dividing the things that were said from the fogginess of the drink. I wait until she satisfies herself that my interpretation could be the true one before raising the delicate issue of how a case might be paid for.

Not wishing to be too upfront, I say, but the people who've approached me before are in rather desperate financial situations and the proceedings won't be cheap.

She has some ideas about crowdfunding, highlighting the injustice that has already occurred against the Smiths and the injustice that could follow for others in their position. Her husband, she tells me, is a whizz at social media, and knows how to get people on his side.

It's a slightly irregular method of employment, but with the case taking shape so clearly, I decide to move with the times and agree.

*

The short time in a cell left me.

There's a message, says Gavin, on your mobile.

I slowly lift my arm but can't quite

He helps to close my hand around the phone, and motions at me to put it to my ear.

I'm looking at him and listening to a recorded message from Pewter, Leghorn and Stock. I feel exhausted.

Well? he asks.

Something about a meeting, I say, as he takes the phone from me and puts it to his ear.

None of this is real. The children are confused by the changes that have been going on, and each of us feels isolated from one another. I try to contain my moods, but it's hard to stop snapping when inside there is anger at

Gavin has called the solicitor.

The case isn't ready yet, he says down the phone, but the investigation continues.

There's a pause, while he listens.

Sounds really positive, he says, glancing at me.

In his eyes is the look of it all turning out fine; his ongoing faith in the power of innocence illuminating them. He's untarnished by the brief time in custody. I'm less optimistic.

He asks me to guess what the phone call was about.

I'm in no mood for guessing.

*

Mrs Bardel, says Philip Stock, has been the real lynchpin driving this forward. Thanks to her husband's innovative approach to raising funds, I am confident that it will be possible to overturn suspicion of each person gathered here.

He explains that the police have made zero progress on the source of the blackmail and can identify no clear pattern directing them to an individual or single entity. There is similarly nothing that can be pinned to Garages-4-Rent, or other websites they've been running under different names. The only person who provides a link between us and the movement of criminal funds is the estate agent.

What about the garage tenants? I ask.

They disappeared into the ether, he says, after the sales went through. So –

You're suggesting we implicate Simon, I say, to save ourselves.

Gavin is looking embarrassed. It's the straight talking he hates; he'd rather be cushioned in politeness. He's not the only one, the gathered eyes are looking around the room, seeking a spokesperson. They rest on Mrs Bardel.

He was careless to allow these sales, she says, and it's possible he really is at the centre.

I tell her it's ridiculous to be proving someone else's guilt when the person is innocent. She launches into a story about her encounter with him. Then argues she witnessed a side to him in the pub that wasn't free of guilt.

The law is complicated, says Philip, and the police have the bit between their teeth as you know first-hand Mrs Smith. And I'm as willing to bet as they are that the proceeds of crime are at the heart of this . . .

Philip's approach is to deflect attention onto Simon.

To do otherwise could take years, he says, which will either be spent inside courtrooms or else imprisoned waiting for appeal after appeal.

Does that matter if it's the right thing? I ask.

There is a collective sigh around me.

Bringing a case against Garages-4-Rent would be like fighting a ghost, says Philip. They'll most likely close up shop and reappear as something else.

Gavin suggests we have some time to talk among ourselves and decide on the right thing to do. But talking with the others makes no difference, they can see no possible reason to jeopardise the freedom of the group in favour of a single individual. Gavin knows this, he's only called the debate to appease me.

He's a nice guy, says Mrs Farleigh, but there's too much for us to lose.

Philip is pleased when he hears the decision and promises to push forward.

I allow my lack of opposition to expose Simon to the full force of Philip's legal team.

*

They start work on a narrative. The estate agent in their tale is an exploiter of the garage scam. He is the frontman for a shell company, and the middleman for money launderers. The team add creative flourishes, a story that he started small as a loner but was annoying the people in charge of the bigger operation. Threats to his family were issued and he was persuaded to work for the larger organisation. This annoyed the smaller time crooks who in turn delivered their own threats. But Simon being an asset to the bigger operation was protected.

It is certainly imaginative and gives the jury some excitement. Philip tells us it was pivotal in Simon being prosecuted. For me it was a bit too dramatic, but each month when my thoughts turn to the estate agent, triggered by the income from the garage arriving in our bank account, and the payments to our landlord going out, I persuade myself that the narrative holds a little bit more truth than it did the month before.

POEMS SPILL

a promise and a whisper –
a nothing yet a hint of something
caught in the flash of syllables
slipping like sunlight off your smile,

a nothing yet a hint of something
the way your lips stroke the words
slipping like sunlight off your smile
till I am giddy with fear and love

the way your lips stroke the words,
my thoughts spin a crazy dance
till I am giddy with fear and love,
offer you the wind and stars.

My thoughts spin a crazy dance
and poems spill that promise all,
offer you the wind and stars
till you still them with a sudden kiss,

and poems spill that promise all
caught in the flash of syllables
till you still them with a sudden kiss,
a promise and a whisper.

VALENTINE

Back bent by the thought and stoop,
my eyes flit over shelves of forgottens,
through junkshops and market venders,
bootfayres and auctions
searching for box, trunk, ammo crate -
a man on a mission amongst
the broken and lick-n-promised,
trawling someone's donated heritage
through a town of up-skillers and charities,
or in Sunday carparks
tiptoeing my way
round exhaust filled puddles,
hopping between patch-worked rafts, tarpaulins
of hope,
plumbing the darkness under trestles
fingers probing damp collapses of cardboard
and on through the week –
trying to make sense of the church-hall jumbles,
disturbing the must of dust yet
busily fishing to pull something solid
from the purged and feng-shuied,
I eschew more obvious, poundshop solutions,
walk away from Argos tiny pen purchase of
stackable storage with airtight lids,
choosing instead to mine
the handleless and battered,
travelled and charred,
seeking a diamond from the rust,
something used but unique
to up-end and bang clear,
wipe clean and buff,

VALENTINE

creating a place to put away
all that was before it's too late,
arranging and boxing, strapping or locking,
to store the ever present past of you and us,
and stall its turning from love to hate.

I have a serious case of you –
but it's time to put it away.

HAIR

Your hair takes advantage of the moment
to interrupt our conversation, everything arrested
by your left hand searching for some word.

A blackbird on a branch stops pecking.
A child's ball hovers mid arc.
The fountain stands still.

You tap the table,
unravel your hair,
It's why we're here, you say.

The blackbird blinks,
the ball bounces,
the fountain cascades.

I finally agree.

GUST

do you remember when you could run?
not just to the corner for some lost box, ingredient,
missed off a list, or a burst down the grass track,
plimsolls yomping mole hills, white lines dusting
in your wake, lungs fit to split all for the sake
of cheers, gold star, pat on the back –
but rather, on and on,
up hills, down dips, scalping the dog yards,
arse-sliding landfill, skish, skishing fields,
that taken risk of hacking into booby traps
of divots, cans and wiry, littering allsorts,
hurdling everything higher than an ankle
lower than a branch with the confidence
of the not yet seriously injured,
feeling with every pass the slightest whippy flick
or gust on neck and knees,
with each pumped fist, shot-out leg
imagining film beaming, rolling silent, fast,
every rush and hurl to your mind's eye
some statuesque, conker-shine thoroughbred
ripping round the coast, oblivious to cliff,
no brakes on the lip, as you fly the patched tarmac,
all day, every day, forever going first, forwards,
to the places where in became out of earshot
and range, past the marks of must return,
those Checkpoint Charlies of Mum's mind
and sure flung, index finger gesture,
safe distance the objective yet seldom mapped,
times not forgotten in the act or ignored
just blurred a bit, so the call-in from the back door
was maybe, almost, never heard.
Don't you ever wish you could run like that?

DANCING STAR

Not exactly Anna Pavlova
but she danced a mean reel.
A nineteenth-century-twirler,
crossing the bog of harsh times
and stepping it out to take
the Irish Sea by storm.

Stepping it out still:
filmic now. Frame on frame
being screened in the brain,
where, star of ancestral foot-tapping,
she runs the gamut of neural noise;
ceilidh-pacing to corner the cortex

hemisphere to hemisphere,
chasséing the corpus callosum
– neither right nor left
neither wrong nor right –
just dancing out of the mind
and into the air around me.

And I am on my feet already
setting about to applaud her.

CUBAN SOUL

Lead guitars jump over congas,
frame Cesar's romantic songs, draw
this audience into sensuous mood.
Strings direct our feet but djembes
compel our bodies to beat with fire.
"Take us to dance in Havana".

Young men with sideburns sit proudly
on the *Malecon,* play guitars
to women who whirl flared skirts,
sing with their melodious bodies.
Beside them, waves pound the rocks.
Old American cars,
you could set up home in, pass by;
their chrome trims shone with devotion.
Old popcorn machines sit outside
next to palm trees.
Trumpets and djembes proclaim
the Cuban flag nailed to a door
in *Churruga.* Posters solicit us
to tune in to 104 fm.
Sunburnt fishermen walk past,
their day's catch detained on their lines;
salty sweat and fish fill the air.
Ancient arches and balconies,
in need of repair, throw shadows
onto neglected sidewalks.

JA-KYUNG OH AT THE ORGAN

Lubeck, August 2013

She comes from a divided nation, North and South,
to a nation once divided East and West,
with only her talent and her uncertain English to
    accompany her,
to play the great organ at St Jacob's,
a mariners' church full of Baltic light.

She is hidden once she has flitted,
barely noticed, across the chancel to the organ loft,
tiny at the centre of the machinery of sound,
so we do not see if she smiles with pleasure at her
    bravery,
to travel so far, to attempt so much,
or frowns at the labour of what she does.

The organ has as many voices as it has pipes.
She commands them to the service of the music,
summons us with thunder,
raises a single note above the others,
intertwining, underpinning,
surrenders us to the convolutions of the Baroque,
tempting us to drowse . . .

until, in one vibration of the gathered air,
harvesting its whole power,
she draws the voices together,
and she and Buxtehude utter a shout of jubilation,
many-tongued,
a comprehension of the unity of all.

She takes no bow, but if you had lingered,
you would have seen her appear
through the same small door she had entered by,
in a black tunic, her hair coiled and pinned,
neat and demure, concealing the wilder sister
who had crashed those final chords.
And, yes, she was smiling in embarrassed triumph
as she shook the hands of her European hosts,
yet withdrawing her fingers as if still raw from the stops
    and keys,

while her music continues to reverberate,
travelling through the ringing air,
out beyond the city and the coast, unheard,
widening like the sky,
where the Baltic opens to the multiplicity of the
    sea-lanes
and the ships pass effortless across frontiers
and the compass-points mean nothing but themselves.

ROBERT FRANK: PRAIRIE MAILBOX

Perhaps it's as empty as the licked can
that carried peaches for Thanksgiving
but more likely a carpet of cicada husks
cushions a pulped birthday card
for the five year old son
who sank in the silt of the Mekong

at night it whistles
at dawn it breathes
as a woman's second best skirt
brushes the tall grass

somewhere behind wormed clapboard
beyond the flyblown screen
a crib with missing bars rocks
and hanging above the rusted bed
a key

'THE KID WHO GOT THROUGH EQUITY'

A work of fiction graced by the occasional truth

The characters and events in this book are
wholly fictional and a product of the author's
imagination. Any resemblance to people living
or dead is entirely and completely coincidental.

All mistakes are my own and generally always have been.

Apart from 'How Much is that Doggy in the Window'
the song that probably kicked it all off was called 'The
First Time' by Adam Faith and the Roulettes. I have loved
it ever since.

DEAD MAN

'So you want a set of drums?' a nod from me and a flurry
of explanation. 'Oh . . . you've already seen some. Where?'
  'A shop on Monument' I gushed 'near the old church.'
  'How much?' He was told. 'Are they gold plated, son?' I
waited, tense. 'Alright' grinned my father a beat later as he
slowly sawed through his steak. 'This is how we get the
money . . .'
  I was driven through a soggy Sunday night to digs in a
street called Pomeroy, an artery of Tiger Bay, Cardiff.
Already in residence were my maternal grandfather and
youngest uncle. 'Welcome' the landlady said as she smiled,
her false teeth dropping a tad 'welfome to my houth.'
  'Hell o son' said grandpa 'and how is leafy ol' Brum?'
  'Still there.'
  I had seen a Gigster blue sparkle drum kit in a second-
hand shop. The price was forty-five pounds and a small
fortune. Being a Dead Man would pay for it. One way or

another a deceased chap's employment details, National
Insurance number, etc find their way to those interested in
such things and part of the fiddle for a busy area supervisor
was to have a ready supply of these 'men' to make up his
wages. Let's say he has thirty working on site, he can, if
there is a willing helper have at least five 'dead' as well. Five
cash pay packets a week. A hundred a month sorts the help
and the rest helps the super with 'expenses' or . . .a son
who wants a pricey drum kit. There's an added advantage
in that 'dead men' don't talk, not if they want to stay
healthy.

'All you have to do is to make the tea and keep your
mouth shut 'said the foreman, a stout red faced Dubliner.
'D'ya understand, young man? I nodded. 'You can of
course make the tay?'

'Yeah' I replied. Break time came and went with no
complaints. That is no complaints about the tea. '

'So . . .you've cum up from Birmingham to help us paint
this gas 'older?' asked a painter from Newcastle.

'I'm sure you don't need any, mister' I said but made no
eye contact.

'Is there anything wrong here' my uncle, Brendon gently
inquired of the sitting little man.

'Nooo . . . no-no' replied the little Geordie. 'I just wanted
to know about this young chap and why e's 'ere.'

'He is here the same as you are . . . to work . . . not to
ask questions . . . got that?'

'No offense meant my friend, no offense' I say. 'It's just
that . . .well, a body likes to know who's who.'

'Curiosity killed the cat, cunt' replied Brendon as he
pushed the guy off the paint tin he was sitting on 'gas
holders are high.' Geordie sat crotch soaked in a brown
brew that was not Newcastle. The kick to his balls did little
to ease his position. 'Any more from you' added my uncle,
'may result in instant and indeed very, painful, dismissal.
Do you savvy, kiddo?'

Story ends

My landlady had some unusual pets. One was a border

collie who was fair and not black and white as they usually are. This was the only four-legged creature I have ever seen that walked sideways all the time, her body seemingly a mixture of emotions, all conflicting and she would gaily follow me to work until I shooed her away. There was another dog but this chap was very old. I would occasionally sit and watch his futile attempts to climb onto the couch (only to slide back down to cold tile). The poor bugger would go through this pantomime several times until somebody tired of the act helped him up to his comforts. There was also a black cat with one eye and so many scars on its face that it looked like an ordinance survey map. To bait this poor battered critter was a mean-eyed, quick witted budgie whose chest was totally bald and when they were in close proximity (which was often as puss regularly tried to end the torture) the room could be a circus.

'Butch . . . (the black cat)' said Gwyneth, the landlady as she sat knitting 'is the local hard knock round 'ere.'

'Yeah' she (she?) can beat 'em all' added Davina, her comely daughter, whose bouncing bust I was staring at. There was silence for a bit then came 'Shirley Bassey used to live just up the road h'you know.'

'Really?'

'Yeah . . . a true Tiger Bay girl she wass.'

'Was she?'

'Yes, and a right little sod, too . . .but she's made good, can't say fairer than that can you. Once she got out she never came back. I wish I had 'er money.'

'I suppose.'

'All that dosh and them lovely clothes and all she sings about is (stands and spreads arms out wide) 'I who 'ave nothin'.' Her mother smiled broadly at this.

'Good voice though' I said.

'Bitch' said my grandfather suddenly 'your cat just bit me, Gwyneth.'

'Ohhhh, she's justa playin'.'

'I wish she'd go play with the traffic' he replied, rubbing the spot which was profusely bleeding. 'I'll need a drink I think' he said 'to get over the pain.' At this Gwyneth smiled then stood and went to get her coat which was crimson and new and made of good wool. As he slipped into his old smother he looked at me and said 'and where will you be going tomorrow (a Saturday)?'

'The castle, then mebbe the flicks, granda' was the smiled but dry reply as the cat looked on knowing I was lying.

I awoke to the silence of an empty house and ten o'clock. Sheila the collie looked up as I entered the back kitchen. I petted her poor head and she sighed. For breakfast I had some corn flakes and cold milk. Butch shook herself and wandered in. 'Hello fuckwit' I yelled knowing full well that Welsh cats can't or simply won't speak English . . .

The weather was warm, a soft breeze stirring white lace curtain as I studied the local newspaper. Where, what shall I go, see? 'Ohhh yes . . . that will do, *The Virgin . . . and the Gypsy*.' At this point Butch made another attempt on the budgie but failing fell backwards, landed hard on a brass companion set which collapsed, its noise was discordant and blue. The cat lay still for a while, deep breathing, her pride (I suppose) suppressing great gobs of pain that she eventually decided to lick. 'If at first you don't succeed?' I said brightly. The animal scowled at me as it limped to seek solace in its usual bowl of mush, only to find the collie fast scoffing it. Thus began a violent struggle and I left for happier climes.

I walked to town and shopped for a bit, trying on trousers at a place that must have catered for the starving, judging by how tight the legs were.

'They like them drainpipes round 'ere' the assistant said, 'the tighter . . . the better.'

'My circulation couldn't stand it mate, sorry.'

I meandered on and around for a while checking out the girls but as I did not know the form for pulling went to the pictures as planned . . .

It was an art house sort of place with vivid posters in different languages. *The Virgin and the Gypsy* thankfully, was in English, photographs in black and white showing its

stars in moody poses. Franco Nero's eyes, piercing and
bright, hypnotically holding his love interest as firmly as
Dracula's teeth. Traffic lazily buzzed as I entered the foyer,
the shade taking a beat to get used to. A middle aged
woman sat in a glazed wooden ticket booth filing her nails
as sunlight bled through old stained glass and the smell of
pine scented industrial disinfectant lingered.

'What will it bee young man?'

'The Vir chin and the umm . . . missis.' A whisper.

'What . . . what's that again?'

'The Vir gin . . . ahem . . . and the Gypsy' cough
'please.' A sly look each way.

Loud as if near deaf 'The Virgin and the what?' A small
queue was forming and folk began to shuffle. 'Picture
staarts soon . . .what's keepin' 'im?' an old man said to no-
one.

'What do you want to see' said the box office woman. . .
'young man? Do speak up.' She asked knowing full well
what I wanted.

'Yeah . . . we'd all like to know your perversions boyo'
said the old boy.

'The Franco Nero one' I said, loud and clear. 'Fuck you
lot' muttered.

'Ohh right.' She eyed me.

'How much is that?'

'A shilling.'

'Take English money?'

'If it's real.'

'Got the Queen's head on it.'

'Just so long as it hasn't got her arse.' At this she started
to laugh, nay quiver like a jelly.

I put down my dosh. 'Thanks.'

'Don't mention it.'

I bought an orange lolly and toffee popcorn in a box big
enough for two and found a seat. Adverts rolled, then the
Pathe News, dada da da dadadada dada dadada dadadada.
'In France Charles DeGaulle presents his case . . .'

'That's a lot of popcorn for one small chap' he said.

I looked around to see a man of perhaps forty.

'Hummm.' I nodded, my mouth too full to respond.

'I haven't seen you here before . . .have you been here before?' I indicated 'no' with a shake of the head.

'I don't come much . . . just on a Saturday . . . not a lot to do on a Saturday in Caardifff.' Again I nodded. After five minutes he tapped me on the shoulder. 'I say . . . do you mind if I sit with you?'

By now I had lost the taste for popcorn and was getting angry.

I turned to him. 'I want to watch the film by myself, OK?'

'Finefine, absolutely fine by me . . . quite right . . . can't watch and talk.'

'Yes.'

The credits rolled.

It was actually very good. There was little in it to call it a sex film, sure there was danger and sexual tension but it was not smut. I think to be honest it was more a treat for women, what with Franco and that. I got up to go. The hand tapped me again. 'Would you like to have a drink with me?'

'No, I don't drink with strangers.'

'We're not strangers we've spoken already.'

'You spoke to me. I have not conversed with you.'

'Just some coffee.'

'No.'

'I waited until the film was finished' he shivered.

Without looking directly at him I knew this was trouble.

'Leave me alone or you will regret it.' I said.

'You led me on . . . now you want to go.'

'If you don't fuck off there will be soapy.'

'Soapy?'

'Soapy bubble, trouble, got it?

'Shit . . . that's what you are . . . shite.'

'FUCK OFF'

'What's happening here?' said a torch.

'This freak is trying to chat me up, that's what's happening.'

The torch moved to the man, lighting his face.

86

'You again' the woman growled, 'get out this instant or it's the police.'

He ran, buttoning his coat as he went. 'I'll see you . . . I'll fuckin' see you' he shrieked, I suppose at me.

'Did he try anything son, did he . . . ?' she asked.

'No, but I've a feeling he wanted to.'

'My goodness, what must you think of us' said another.

RENEWAL

A woman sits on Whitstable beach
she ponders the damage of last night's storm:
heaped pebbles, a battered boat,
and a rusty winch
           abandoned.

The ebb tide has exposed
an expanse of sand where rivulets trickle
and quartz glints in the sun;
she squints, wipes salt tears from her face,
turns her head at a screech
like the crank of a winch – a gull
                swoops

across tired whispering waves
on relentless return, they'll wash
and rewash the shore, cover
the scars imposed by the storm;

she knows the boat can be mended –
it's time to move on.

WOOLPIT CHILD

My brother never thrived
though I was always the greener
he folded back into a wooden pod
and we planted him root down

I battled the wind's fetch
in that first loneliness
as the sun sharpened its edge
on this too-bright land

learned to make a virtue
of my body's strange sap
curled men's hands
around my dankness

set out to find dew hollows
in one white throat
to breed him a son
and a daughter

then faded to olive
under the skin's web

Made in the USA
Middletown, DE
17 July 2023

34783005R00057